JUDY MOODY AND FRIENDS
Not-So-Lucky Lefty

Megan McDonald

illustrated by Erwin Madrid

based on the characters
created by Peter H. Reynolds

CANDLEWICK PRESS

For all the lucky lefties

M. M.

To my wife, Hoài

E. M.

Text copyright © 2018 by Megan McDonald
Illustrations copyright © 2018 by Peter H. Reynolds
Judy Moody font copyright © 2003 by Peter H. Reynolds

Judy Moody®. Judy Moody is a registered trademark of Candlewick Press, Inc.

First edition 2018

Library of Congress Catalog Card Number 2018935019
ISBN 978-0-7636-9605-4 (hardcover)
ISBN 978-0-7636-9847-8 (paperback)

18 19 20 21 22 CCP 10 9 8 7 6 5 4 3 2

Printed in Shenzhen, Guangdong, China

This book was typeset in ITC Stone Informal.
The illustrations were created digitally.

Candlewick Press
99 Dover Street
Somerville, Massachusetts 02144

visit us at www.candlewick.com

CONTENTS

CHAPTER 1
Lucky Lefty and Mighty Righty

"One, two, three, four, I declare a thumb war." Stink dipped his thumb. He was too quick; Judy couldn't catch him.

Her little brother sure was good at thumb-wrestling. Judy just had to beat him. "Tell me again why I have to do this left-handed?" Judy asked.

"Tomorrow is August thirteenth. If you want to celebrate Left Handers Day with me and Dad," said Stink, "you have to beat me like a southpaw. That means left-handed."

Judy dipped, dived, and dodged Stink's thumb.

Sneak attack! All of a sudden, Stink faked her out, slid his thumb sideways, then—*ka-blam*—pinned her thumb down.

"I win! I win!" Stink spun around the room. "Winner, winner, chicken dinner!"

Wait just a southpaw second. "You have to hold my thumb down for three seconds," said Judy. "That was not three seconds."

"Was too," said Stink. "I beat you fair and square with Lucky Lefty here."

Judy wiggled her right hand. "I could beat you thumbs-down if you let me use Mighty Righty."

"You mean the right hand of doom? Lefties rule all!"

"What's so great about being left-handed, anyway?" Judy asked.

"Left-handers are creative. Left-handers are geniuses. Left-handers are presidents! Einstein was a lefty. Kermit the Frog is a lefty. Half of all cats are lefties."

Mouse batted her squeak toy with her left paw. *Traitor!* Even Judy's cat was left-handed.

Judy was feeling left out.

Judy wanted to be creative. Judy wanted to be a genius. Judy wanted to be a president. But most of all, Judy wanted to go with Stink and Dad on their Left Handers Day visit to the pretzel factory.

"C'mon, Stink," said Judy. "Give me another chance."

"Okay, here's a test."

"What kind of test?" asked Judy.

"Scratch your nose," said Stink.

Judy scratched her nose.

"Open the door," said Stink. Judy opened the door.

"Write your name," said Stink. Judy wrote her name.

"High five!" said Stink. Judy high-fived Stink.

"Your test is complete," said Stink.

"That's it? Awesome! I get an A for *Amazing!*"

"You get an F for *Flunked.* You used your right hand every single time. You even high-fived me with your right hand of doom."

"ROAR!" said Judy. "You tricked me."

"See? Being left-handed is harder than you think," said Stink.

"I just need a little practice."

Stink sighed and handed Judy a piece of paper and a pair of left-handed scissors. "Let's see you cut out a circle with your left hand."

"Easy-peasy mac-and-cheesy," said Judy. But it was not so easy-peasy. Her left hand wouldn't behave. She felt like a preschooler. She held up her circle at last. *GULP!*

"Was your circle chewed by a great white shark or something?" Stink asked.

"Or something."

Judy read Stink's T-shirt: LIVE LIFE LEFT. She tried to write it on one of her old T-shirts with her left hand. It looked like LOVE LAF LEAF.

"See?" said Judy. "I can do stuff left-handed."

"Fine," said Stink, "you can come with me and Dad to It's Raining Pretzels tomorrow on one condition: you have to be left-handed the whole entire day."

Judy did not want to be left out. Judy wanted to have triple fun with Stink and Dad.

"You're on." Judy raised her left hand in the air. "I, Judy Moody, do solemnly swear to be left-handed for one whole entire day."

CHAPTER 2
Pretzilla

The next morning, Judy opened her
left eye.

Happy Left Handers Day!

Judy brushed her hair left-handed.
She looked like an electric eel. Judy
brushed her teeth left-handed. She got
toothpaste up her nose. Judy pulled
on her shirt left-handed. She fell flat
on the floor.

Yikes. At this rate, Judy was not going to be president of the Creative Geniuses and Cats Club any time soon.

"All aboard the Lefty Express," called Dad.

Judy raced Stink to the car. *Oops!*
She *almost* opened the door with her
right hand.

She tried to buckle her seat belt left-handed, but she got as twisted up as an octopus in an ocean of yarn.

"Help!"

Stink untwisted her.

Judy smoothed out her shirt. All
the way to It's Raining Pretzels, Judy
squeezed a ball in her left hand.
Open, shut, open, shut.

"What are you doing?" Stink asked.
"Making my left hand stronger,"
said Judy.

At the shop, there were pretzel rods, sticks, and twists. Blue pretzels, frozen pretzels, mustache pretzels, pretzels that spelled words. A sign said THE WORLD'S BIGGEST PRETZEL WEIGHS 1,728 POUNDS!

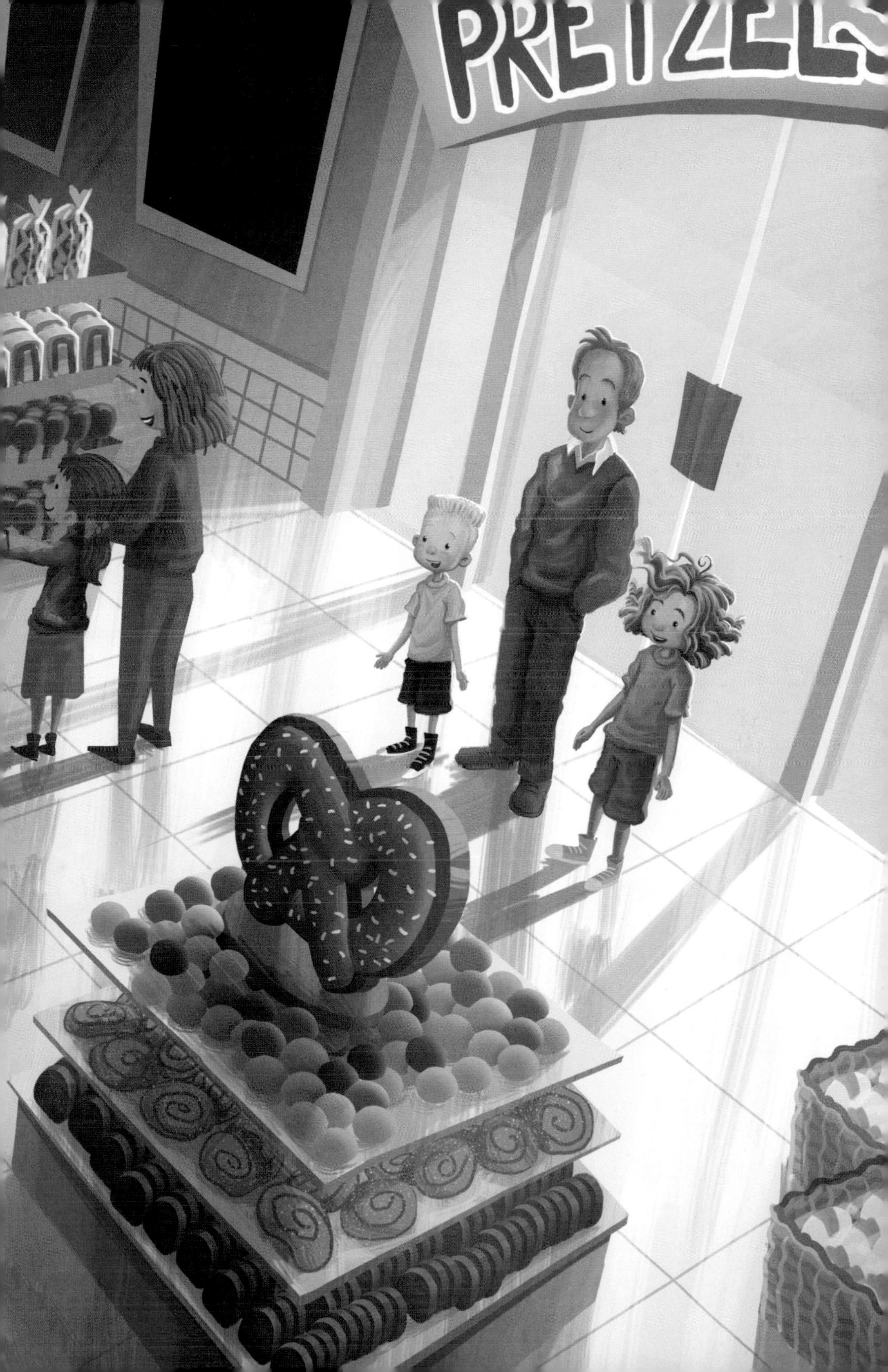
PRETZELS

"How about a snack first," said Dad. "Hot dogs in pretzel buns?"

"And hot cocoa," said Stink. "We can dip our pretzels."

Judy went to reach for a green Alien Pretzel. Stink held his pretzel mustache under his nose. "Pretzel police! You're under arrest for using your right hand."

Judy stopped just in time. *Phew!* That was a close one. She raised her *left* hand. "I solemnly swear to obey the Law of the Left for the rest of the day."

When Judy used her left hand to squeeze ketchup on her hot dog, it squirted all over her.

"You look like a zombie!" Stink cried.

When Judy took a bite of hot dog, it shot out of the bun and landed in Stink's lap.

When Judy tried to pick up her
cocoa left-handed, she knocked it
over.

After their snack, Judy and Stink
went on a pretzel hunt. They made
their own pretzels. They even played
pretzel Twister.

"Hey, look," said Dad, pointing to the activity room. "Who wants to build a pretzel roller coaster?"

"Last one there is pickled pretzel poop!" called Stink.

Tables with bowls of pretzels lined the room.

"Let's make our coaster shaped like an upside-down pretzel," said Judy.

Dad sketched it on a napkin.

"Here's a double-reverse coaster . . ."

"With bat wings," added Stink.

Judy and Stink worked on a ramp made of mini-waffle pretzels. Dad used pretzel rods to hold up the first loop. Judy tried to add a pretzel to the loop. *Oops-a-daisy!* She bumped Stink, making him knock over the ramp.

"You wrecked it!" cried Stink.

"Me? *You* wrecked it," said Judy.

"*You* bumped *me*," said Stink.

"Stink, how about if we let Judy use her right hand for this?" said Dad.

"NO!" said Judy. "I have to be a lefty *all day*."

"Then no more fighting," said Dad.

"I'll do the pretzels," Stink said to Judy. "You stick to the glue."

Judy picked up the glue. She tried to make a dot. It came out a blob. She tried to make a line. It came out a glob. She tried to make a squiggle. It came out a giant gloopy glob of goop!

For the next hour, Judy and Stink stacked pretzels every which way.

Their coaster was more glue than pretzel.

"Pretzilla!" said Stink.

"*Glue*-zilla!" said Judy.

Judy, Stink, and Dad went around admiring the other pretzel coasters. When they got back to their table, Pretzilla had a ribbon on its name tag.

"We won?!" cried Stink.

"Each coaster gets a special ribbon," said Dad.

"What did we win for?" asked Judy. "Most glue?"

"Most creative name," said Dad.

"Lefties rule!" cried Stink.

"Yeah we do," said Judy. She high-fived Stink and Dad with her left hand.

Dad waved tickets in the air. "For making a coaster, we get free passes to play goony golf."

"Can we, can we, can we?" asked
Judy and Stink.

"Let's go!" said Dad.

CHAPTER 3
The Ultimate Left-Handed, High-Flying Hole in One

Judy, Stink, and Dad sang all the way to the goony-golf place. They sang the purple people eater song at the top of their lungs.

Stink saw it first. "There it is!" The giant purple-people-eater statue greeted them in front of the mini-golf course.

"The purple people eater's still here!" said Dad. "Do you kids know that this is where I brought Mom on our first date?"

"For real?" asked Judy.

"No way!" said Stink.

"True story," said Dad. "We played glow-in-the-dark goony golf till midnight and sipped a root-beer float from the same straw."

"Gross!" said Stink.

Stink asked for an orange left-handed golf club. "My putter is called The Orange Crush because I am so going to crush you."

Judy made a face. Dad chose a blue club. "Why don't you get a right-handed putter, Judy?"

"The day isn't over. I can't give up on being a lefty now." Judy picked up a left-handed purple putter.

The goony-golf course was full of
windmills and waterfalls, spiderwebs
and shipwrecks. When they got to the
first green, Stink tapped the ball into
the hole in two strokes. "Par two!"

Then Judy was up. Tap. Judy's ball rolled a few inches. Tap. The ball plinked off the edge.

Tap.

Tap.

Tap.

Tap.

Score!

"It took Judy six tries!" cried Stink. "The Orange Crush rules."

"It's hard being a lefty," said Judy.

"It is," agreed Dad, "but you'll get the hang of it."

"Yeah, after about seven years!" said Stink.

Judy swung, swatted, and swooshed her way through the first nine holes. Stink only had to duck twice when Judy's ball zinged sideways.

"The Orange Crush is crushing you!" Stink cried.

They came to the next hole. "This time, hit the ball a little harder," Dad told Judy. "Give it some speed."

Swoosh! Judy's ball went singing through the air and landed—*PLOP*—in the middle of Pirate Pond.

"It's a sinker. You'll have to ask for another ball," called Stink.

Judy slumped. "When is *Right Handers Day?*" she grumped.

"Every single day of the year," Stink and Dad said at the very same time.

"Same-same!" said Judy. She ran off to get a new ball.

When she came back, Stink was on hole thirteen. "Hey, it's my turn," said Judy.

"Nah-uh," said Stink. "You still have to finish the snake hole."

"Stink, let's cut Judy a break," said Dad.

"Yeah, Stinker. This could be my first hole in one."

Stink snorted.

Judy hit the ball hard. The ball sped down the green, soared loop-de-loop through a metal shoot, and spun in circles around the hole.

Judy held her breath. The ball stopped . . . right *next* to the hole.

"Ooh," said Dad. "So close!"

The next hole was a haunted house. Ghosts gave Stink the goose bumps. Skeletons gave Stink the shivers. He skipped ahead and drove his ball through a giant pair of glasses.

"Hey, Cheater Pants," called Judy. "You skipped a hole."

"Haunted houses give me the creeps," said Stink.

"Lefties scare easy," said Judy. "True fact."

"Maybe we do," Dad said, laughing.

"Do not!" called Stink. But he still skipped the haunted house.

Judy putted her way through
a pyramid, a sea monster, and a
Chinese dragon. At last she caught
up to Stink at hole eighteen.

Stink made his last shot. "The Orange Crush is over and out. Dad, can I get a root-beer float?" Dad made his trying-to-decide-if-Stink-can-have-sugar face.

"Like you and Mom," said Stink. "C'mon. It's Left Handers Day!"

Stink ran to the window and came back with a big frothy drink. He slurped it at the picnic table next to hole eighteen.

Dad made the shot in two strokes. "Now you try. Really put your arm into it."

"So I have to hit the ball uphill *and* sink it in one of those holes in the shipwreck?" Judy asked.

"Yes. The last hole's the hardest," said Dad. "Get a hole in one here and your name goes up on the Wall of Honor."

Judy took a swing and *wheee!* The ball shot up the ramp.

The ball flew over the shipwreck. The ball sailed through the air and landed with a *kerplunk*. But it didn't plop in the pond this time.

"HEY!"

It crash-landed, *splash*-landed, dead center in the middle of Stink's root-beer float!

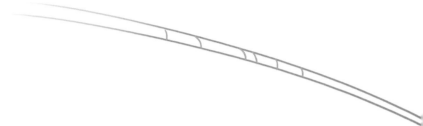

"Vol-ca-no!" yelled Stink as root-
beer float erupted and oozed all over.
"It's a sinker, Stinker!" called Judy.
"Hole in one!" called Dad.

"Sorry about the root-beer bath, Stinkerbell."

"What's the final score, Dad?" Stink asked.

"Oh, I was supposed to keep score?"

"Dad, no way! The Orange Crush squashed The Purple Putter!"

"You may have won the *goony-golf game,* Stink," said Judy, "but I used my *left hand* all day."

Ding-ding-ding-ding-ding! Just then, a bell rang. A man in a goony-golf shirt came running. "That's the wildest hole-in-one shot I've ever seen. This young lady gets her name on the High-Flying, Purple-People-Eater Hole-in-One Wall of Honor. And a free root-beer float!"

"For real?" Judy squealed.

Dad put his arms around them both. "My two silly southpaws."

"Live life left!" yelled Stink.

"Love laf leaf!" yelled Judy.